Christmas COOKIES

Bite-Size Holiday Lessons

written by

Amy Krouse Rosenthal

illustrated by

Jane Dyer

HarperCollins*Publishers*

Christmas Cookies: Bite-Size Holiday Lessons
Text copyright © 2008 by Amy Krouse Rosenthal
Illustrations copyright © 2008 by Jane Dyer
Manufactured in China.

Library of Congress Cataloging-in-Publication Data is available.
ISBN 978-0-06-058024-7 (trade bdg.) — ISBN 978-0-06-058025-4 (lib. bdg.)

Typography by Rachel Zegar
1 2 3 4 5 6 7 8 9 10
❖
First Edition

*When cooking, it is important to keep safety in mind. Children should always ask
permission from an adult before cooking and should be supervised by an adult in the
kitchen at all times. The publisher and authors disclaim any liability from any injury that
might result from the use, proper or improper, of the recipe contained in this book.*

I dedicate this book to my
sweet friend Kay Murphy.
—A.K.R.

For Brookie, with so many thanks
for helping paint so many cookies.
You are a joy!
—J.D.

ANTICIPATION means,

I've been thinking all day about making the cookies.

I'm so excited. I can't wait.

TRADITION means

each year at the same time we make the same

cookies and wear our special matching aprons.

DISAPPOINTED means,

I tried to make it look like a star,

but it didn't turn out at all the way I expected.

CELEBRATE means

time to get out the sprinkles!

APPRECIATIVE means,

Thank you so so much
for taking the time to bake with me.

PROSPERITY means,

My goodness, just look at all these cookies!

CHARITABLE means

setting a big batch aside to give to people

who maybe don't have any cookies at all.

FOR YOU

RESPONSIBLE means,

You asked me to put away the cookie cutters,
and you can count on me to do it.

MODERATION means
at the party not having twenty cookies,
and not having zero cookies,
but having just enough cookies.

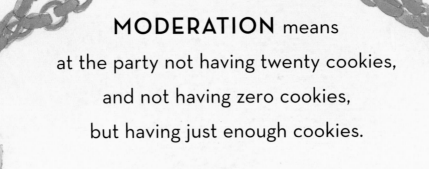

RECIPROCATE means,

Today I'm making cookies at my friend's house.

and then next time I'll invite her to make them at my house.

FRUSTRATED means,

I can't believe we burned them again!

PERSEVERANCE means,

We tried and tried and tried.

and finally we made the perfect not-burned batch.

SELFISH means

grabbing the last cookie without

asking if anyone might want it.

THOUGHTFUL means,

Let's give some to our neighbor!

LONELY means,

The cookie doesn't taste as good
when I eat it by myself.

SHARING means,

Thanks for giving me a taste.
Would you like a bite of mine?

GRATITUDE means

taking a minute to look around the table and be

thankful for all the people and all the cookies.

FAMILY means

enjoying our cookies together.

GRACIOUS means

putting out a plate for our special guest.

BELIEVE means,

I might never see it happen,

but he will come and eat them.

I just know it.

JOY means,

My heart is happy and bright, and mmmmm,
don't you just love the way the house smells?

PEACE means
no one is worried about anyone else's cookie . . .
in this moment we are all quietly content
with the cookies we have.

HOPE means,

I'm filled with good feelings about what will be.

Christmas
COOKIES

INGREDIENTS

$^3/_4$ cup softened butter

1 cup sugar

2 eggs

1 teaspoon vanilla

2 $^1/_2$ cups all-purpose flour

1 teaspoon baking powder

1 teaspoon salt

DIRECTIONS

Mix butter and sugar together and beat in the eggs and vanilla. Add flour, baking powder, and salt, and mix until combined. Chill for two hours.

Roll out a small amount of dough at a time, keeping the rest in refrigerator. Place dough on floured board, cover with a sheet of floured wax paper, and roll until $^1/_8$" thick. Dip cookie cutters into flour to prevent sticking and cut dough into desired shapes. Bake at 350 ºF in a preheated oven for 6–8 minutes until edges are light brown.

Sprinkle with colored sugar.